YELLOW Rabbit

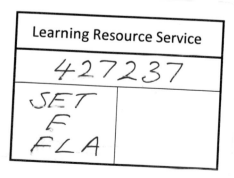

For my dear parents, who hunted tirelessly for my lost yellow rabbit and inspired this tale

Published in 2013 in Great Britain by
Barrington Stoke Ltd
18 Walker Street, Edinburgh, EH3 7LP

www.barringtonstoke.co.uk

This story was first published in a different form in
Wow! 366, Scholastic Children's Books, 2008

Text © 2008 Teresa Flavin
Illustrations © Rich Watson

The moral right of the author has been asserted
in accordance with the Copyright, Designs and
Patents Act 1988

Individual ISBN 978-1-78112-296-9
Pack ISBN 978-1-78112-308-9

Not available separately

Printed in China by Leo

www.barringtonstoke.co.uk

Barrington Stoke

Teresa Flavin

Illustrated by Rich Watson

YELLOW
Rabbit

We were on the way to Madrid airport when my little sister Ashley said, "I left my yellow rabbit at the hotel!"

"We can't go back or we'll miss our plane,"
Dad said. "I'll phone the hotel later."

Ashley sulked.

As soon as we got home, Ashley made Dad call the hotel in Spain. He asked the manager to find Yellow Rabbit and call him back.

"Don't get your hopes up, Ashley," Dad said.
"But maybe we'll be lucky."

Ashley hugged her teddy and sobbed for
Yellow Rabbit.

Back in the hotel, Maria the cleaner found Yellow Rabbit.

When Maria finished work, she sat the rabbit on the table in the staffroom as she left.

No one took any notice of it except for Ramon the handyman.

'I'll have some fun,' he thought.

When Maria, Ana and Beatriz came into work in the morning, Yellow Rabbit had on a top hat made from a cork.

"That rabbit is no boy!" Ana said.

Ana made a dress from a plastic bag and tied it round Yellow Rabbit.

"She needs a crown," Beatriz said. She put a pink scrunchie on Yellow Rabbit's head.

"And jewellery," Maria said. She tied a sparkly earring around Yellow Rabbit's neck.

The next day Ramon made a tiny Spanish hat and flip-flops for Yellow Rabbit.

Beatriz made a frilly Spanish dress.

Ana tied bangles of silver elastic round Yellow Rabbit's arms.

Soon they had made Yellow Rabbit lots of outfits – even a swimsuit and a fur coat.

Every day Ashley asked Dad if the hotel
had called. Every day Dad hugged her and
said no.

Ashley thought Yellow Rabbit was in a skip somewhere. She cried into her teddy's fur.

One day a Christmas card arrived from the hotel. In the photo, the cleaners stood round a yellow rabbit in an elf suit.

Dad rushed to phone the hotel.

A week later, a parcel came for Ashley.
Yellow Rabbit was inside, on top of a
cornflakes box full of outfits.

Yellow Rabbit wore a raincoat over a flamenco dress. There was a paper umbrella and a note in its paws.

Ashley kissed Yellow Rabbit and read the note out loud.

"Thank you for letting your rabbit stay
with us. She missed you! Love, Maria, Ana,
Beatriz and Ramon."

Are you NUTS about stories?

MICHAEL ROSEN
Wolfman

Illustrated by Chris Mou

Pancake Face

Georgia Byng
Illustrated by Mike Phillips

Teresa Flavin
YELLOW Rabbit

Illustrated by Rich Watso

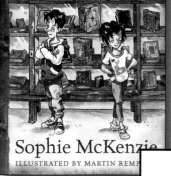

Harry and Kate
at the
Book Museum

Sophie McKenzie
ILLUSTRATED BY MARTIN REMP

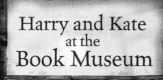

Read ALL the Acorns!